Breakfast at the Zoo

written by Pam Holden
illustrated by Jim Storey

The zoo animals were hungry.
But the zoo keeper was late.
He was asleep in his bed.

"Wake up! You are late,"
cried the hungry animals.
"Give us some breakfast."

But the zoo keeper
did not wake up.

"Wake up! We are hungry," hissed the snakes.
"Come and give us some food."

But the zoo keeper
did not wake up.

"We are hungry. Wake up!"
cried the elephants.
"Give us some breakfast."

But the zoo keeper
did not wake up.

"Wake up! You are late," roared the lions and tigers. "Come and give us some food."

But the zoo keeper did not wake up.

"Wake up! We are hungry.
Give us some breakfast,"
cried the monkeys.

But the zoo keeper did not wake up.

"Wake up! You are late!"
cried the hungry parrots.
"Come and give us some food."

The zoo keeper woke up.

"Here is your breakfast," said the zoo keeper. "I'm sorry I am late!"